Black Mirror

Diane Gonzales Bertrand

SCHOLASTIC INC.

New York   Toronto   London   Auckland   Sydney
Mexico City   New Delhi   Hong Kong   Buenos Aires

Illustrations
Randy Pollak
Models: Thanks to the students of IS 125, NYC
and to The Champions Club

Developed by ONO Books in cooperation with Scholastic Inc.

ISBN 0-439-57922-8

1 2 3 4 5 6 7 8 9 10   23   12 11 10 09 08 07 06 05 04 03

Contents

Welcome to This Book

Do you know any brothers or sisters who get along perfectly? Who never fight? Hmmm. Well, maybe they fight just a little.

Gilbert and Jaime are brothers. But they act more like enemies. Jaime is brainy. Gilbert's more of a jock. It doesn't take much to get these two arguing. Then one day, Gilbert and Jaime have a very strange adventure. And if they keep fighting, they may not make it out alive.

Can these brothers become friends?

Target Words
These words will help you understand Gilbert and Jaime's strange adventure.

- **bargain:** a good price

  Gilbert and Jaime are looking for a bargain at the flea market.

- **path:** a trail or route for walking; a plan for living your life

  Gilbert and Jaime need to find a new path.

- **selfish:** caring only about yourself; not thinking of others

  Gilbert and Jaime learn the price of being selfish.

Reader Tips
Here's how to get the most from this book.

- **Illustrations** Look at the illustrations on pages 11, 15, 24, 32, 43, and 48. As you read, pay attention to details in the pictures. They will help you to better understand what's going on in the story.

- **Theme** A theme is the overall message or idea about life that the author wants to get across to readers. Think about what happens as a result of the character's words and actions—this is usually where you'll find the theme, or moral, of a story.

Mysteries From History

Jaime is always saying stupid stuff like that.

You want it, we've got it. That's what the big white sign outside Perez Flea Market says.

I hung my arm out the window of Uncle Tulio's van. Once again I thought, "That sign's so corny."

My little brother, Jaime, was in the backseat. "We want it, they've got it," he sang out. "So, I wonder what mysteries from history the market has for us today."

Jaime always said dumb stuff like that. He was such a nerd. I wish he had stayed home. Actually, I wish Uncle Tulio had let me stay home alone.

Already a long line of cars was parked along Highway 37. A green wooden fence surrounded the market. Inside were the "mysteries from history." But to me the mystery was why people would buy all that old junk.

People set up big umbrellas and small tents everywhere. There were food stands for tacos, roasted corn, sodas, and candy. A lot of people just sold stuff off the back of their trucks.

Uncle Tulio parked. We got out and followed him through the market. I couldn't believe it. For thirty minutes he made us look for glass doorknobs. Uncle Tulio fixes up old houses. He's good at his job. He's really into details.

Uncle Tulio stopped at yet another table to look around. I whispered to Jaime, "This is so boring. Please! Save me! A doorknob is a doorknob."

"Tell that to Uncle Tulio," Jaime whispered back. He knew I wouldn't.

"Is there a problem, Gilbert?" Uncle Tulio stood up straight. At his full height, he's a **towering** six foot three. I start high school next year. I'm still two heads shorter than him.

Heads Up!

Do you think Gilbert likes going to the flea market? Why or why not?

Jaime is even shorter. He'll start middle school no taller than an ant.

"No, Uncle Tulio," I said, "there's no problem."

Uncle Tulio looked down at his watch. "You know, guys, you should really get busy shopping. You don't have time to follow me around all day."

"Us? Shopping?" I said. "Why do we need to go shopping?"

He frowned at me. "You're the oldest, Gilbert. You should know what tomorrow is."

Jaime put on a big smile. "It's Mother's Day," he said, stamping on my foot hard. Ouch!

I had totally forgotten. I had ten dollars in my pocket. And I had plans for that money. But I knew that Mom did a lot for us. It was especially hard for her now that Dad was away in the army. Still, I didn't want to part with all of my money. Maybe we could find her something nice and cheap. I mean, something that is nice but not too expensive.

"We'll meet up at the front gate," Uncle Tulio said. "Say, about noon?" Then he looked at me with a raised eyebrow. "Gilbert, you and Jaime are going to stick together, right?"

That was his way of warning me not to ditch my brother. I did that a lot. Jaime was a little pest.

"Yeah, fine, Uncle Tulio," I said. "We'll meet you in an hour."

Jaime and I walked off by ourselves. Jaime said, "I have five dollars. How much do you have on you, Gilbert?"

Hmm. Maybe hanging out with the squirt would pay off yet. "I've got two bucks." I figured seven dollars would be plenty for Mom's present.

We walked around and looked at stuff. But we didn't agree on anything. It was hot and I was looking for a place to buy a cold drink for myself. Then I saw this rock **path.** It curved down the hill like a snake.

Where did that come from? I wondered. I had never seen it before.

—Heads Up!—
Why does Gilbert tell Jaime that he has only two dollars? Why doesn't he tell his brother how much he really has?

The path led to a tall tree. A green truck was parked in the shade. Well, at least we could get out of the hot sun for a while.

An old man was standing next to the green truck. His straw hat pointed up like a crown. A striped blanket covered his shoulders. That was weird considering it was about 90 degrees out. He had laid out his things on the tailgate of his truck. I couldn't tell from here what he had for sale. But Mom liked **unique** things. So it was worth a look. Maybe he would have something nice and cheap. I mean . . . oh, you know.

Heads Up!

Do you think the old man will have something that Gilbert will want to buy for his mother? Why or why not?

Jaime and Gilbert head down the path.

2

The Black Mirror

Jamie breaks a snake-bird statue.
And look where it gets us.

"Gilbert, where are you going? It's almost time to meet Uncle Tulio!"

As usual, I ignored my brother. I just walked down the path. "I'm going this way. Come or not." I heard him stumbling on the rocks behind me.

No one else was around. I thought the old guy should have set up in a better place. He probably wasn't selling much. That was fine with me. Maybe he'd give us a **bargain.**

The first thing I saw was a striped blanket. On top of it were some straw birds with black glass eyes. I saw four wooden masks with colored feathers. There was a row of rope drawings glued on wood squares. Two large clay pots were painted in bright colors.

Then there were these clay statues. They had long snake bodies and wide wings.

I picked one up. It felt really weird. The air was hot. But the statue felt cold.

"What is it?" I asked.

"I call it a snake-bird," the old man said. "It's the god Quetzalcóatl."

"Ket-what-sill?" It sounded like something Jaime would know about. And sure enough . . .

"Ket-sal-koh-AHT-ul," said Jaime. He pronounced the word like I was an idiot.

"I knew that," I said.

"Really, then who is he?" my brother said.

"He was . . . Yeah, that's right, he was . . ."

"Quetzalcóatl was an Aztec god," Jaime said, rolling his eyes.

"That's what I was going to say, if you didn't cut me off." Then I punched him in the arm for being so rude.

"So then you know who the Aztecs were, right? They were the people who lived in Mexico long before the Spanish got there in the 1500s. Didn't you learn about it in Spanish class?"

"Sure," I said. "I just forgot."

Jaime kept on talking. "There are a lot of stories about him. He created the world. He changed into animals. He found food to feed his people. And he—"

"Yeah, yeah, yeah." I shook the statue near my brother's nose. "Who cares about that dumb stuff? You little show-off!"

"You're just mad 'cause you don't know anything!" Jaime pushed the statue away from his face.

I lost my grip. I juggled it in my hands. I couldn't hang on. The snake-bird dropped to the rocky path. It broke into four pieces.

"Jaime, look what you did," I said. "You broke the man's statue."

"I didn't break anything. You're the one who dropped it, genius."

"You pushed me, nerd!" I looked at the old man. I wondered what he would say.

Heads Up!

Who do you think is to blame for breaking the statue? Jaime? Gilbert? Or both?

"Jaime, look what you did," Gilbert says. "You broke the man's statue."

"Who's going to pay for my broken statue?" the man asked us.

I shrugged. "My brother will pay for it," I said. "He has all the money."

"No way," Jaime said. His voice got louder. "You have money, too."

"Yeah, but I got plans for my ten bucks," I told him.

"Ten? You said you had two!" Jaime yelled.

"I guess I lied. What are you going to do about it?" I said, staring down at him.

The old man suddenly lifted his arms under his blanket. Jaime ducked. I was about to take off. But all he did was pull out a circle of shiny black stone. It had a short wooden handle. I looked at it again. It was a black mirror. He held it in front of our faces.

"You need to find a better path to walk as brothers," he said.

All of a sudden, I felt this cold wind. Everything went dark.

3

A New Path

**There's nothing "better" about this path.
How do we get out of here?**

Black winds swirled around us. The ground was rocky. I was suddenly freezing. I couldn't see a thing. I put out my hands in front of me. I heard my brother's voice.

"What's happening?" Jaime's voice sounded very faint.

"Where are you?" I tried to open my eyes but the wind stung them. It screamed inside my ears. I felt cold hands grab my T-shirt.

"I'm here," Jaime yelled. "Gilbert, help me!"

I grabbed hold of his skinny body.

We stood together. The hard winds were practically knocking us over.

"I got you. Hang on!" I cried out.

Just then that dark, cold wind stopped

completely. I took a step back. I opened my eyes and blinked a few times.

"Get off me, man," I said and pushed my brother away.

Then I looked around. The old man was gone. His truck was gone. The flea market was gone. Instead I saw tall mountains pointing up to cloudy skies. Thick trees stood all around us.

In front of us was a dirt path snaking through the forest. The cold wind was gone. A warm breeze took its place.

"Where are we?" Jaime turned in a complete circle. "What happened to the flea market?"

I stared up at the gray skies. "I don't know." I had to admit I was a little scared, too. "Maybe the old man did something to us," I said, not knowing what.

"You should have paid him for the statue," Jaime said. "He put us here. Wherever we are!"

"Maybe none of this is real," I said. "Maybe we're both dreaming. Maybe it's still last night and we're asleep."

"What a dumb idea," Jaime said. He reached out. He pinched my arm hard.

"Hey! That hurt!" I was ready to punch him.

"You felt that, right? We aren't in a dream," Jaime said. "Remember what that old man said about a path? Well, we better find that path 'cause it might be the only way out of here."

My little brother was making sense. I don't know how he could think clearly at a time like this, but I guess someone had to. "Okay, Jaime, let's start walking."

I had barely taken a step when something whizzed by my nose. That's when I realized we weren't alone.

Heads Up!

The old man told them to find a better path to walk as brothers. What do you think he is trying to tell them?

4

Ría

Where did this girl come from? Maybe this place isn't so bad after all.

I turned around and saw a girl standing between two trees. She had black hair. Feathers of different colors were woven into it. She seemed to be about my age. She wore a cape of feathers over a white dress. Under all those feathers, she looked kind of cute. I wanted to say something to her. But I noticed that she wasn't smiling.

She was swinging something in her hand. It looked like a slingshot. It held a black stone in it. That must be what went whizzing by me. She looked ready to **sling** another rock.

"Who are you?" she yelled. "And what do you **seek**?"

She spoke funny. But luckily she spoke English. So I smiled big. "Hi, there. I mean, hello.

I am Gilbert. This is Jaime. We are here looking for a better path."

"Are you gods?" she asked.

"No, we are just regular guys," Jaime said. "We're brothers, actually."

Finally, she stopped swinging the slingshot.

"I am Ría," she said. She walked closer to us. "Where are your feathers?"

I looked down at my T-shirt and blue jeans. "These are normal clothes where we live."

Seeing her up close, I could **admire** her. She was pretty. Her face was smooth with small black eyes. She'd be popular at my school.

"Do you live in another village?" she asked.

"Sort of," I said. I didn't know how I could explain it.

"Gilbert, tell her about the old man and the black mirror," Jaime said.

Ría looked shocked. "A black mirror? How

Heads Up!

Look up the word admire. *What does Gilbert admire about Ría?*

can you find yourself in a black mirror?"

Leave it to my dumb brother to upset her.

"Listen, Ría—" I wanted to smooth things over.

"Do you tell me truth or lies?" she said, without letting me finish.

I started to tell her that I never lied.

But she held up her hand. "Don't speak. I will take you to our leader. He will know what to do." Then she turned to walk away.

Jaime and I followed her. Jaime got in front of me but I pushed him out of the way. I wanted to walk next to Ría.

"Ría, what can you tell me about this place?"

"My people are starving," she said. "I'm scared we will all die."

5

Tangled, Inside and Out

"The more you pull, the more it grabs you,"
she says. Maybe that's good advice.

I wanted to ask her more. But I had to **concentrate** on walking. She hopped over roots and vines with no problem. It looked like she had done it a hundred times. I stumbled whenever I didn't think about my feet.

"Gilbert, wait! I'm stuck!" Jaime called out.

I turned around. Jaime's knee was caught between two vines. He tugged. But that only seemed to tangle him up worse.

"Jaime, don't be so lame," I said. "Come on!"

I looked at Ría. "He's just looking for attention. Ignore him."

She gave me a look that kind of reminded me of the old man at the flea market. And then she walked back toward my brother.

"It's a rope plant," says Ría. **"The more you pull, the more it grabs you."**

"It's a rope plant," Ría spoke gently. "The more you pull, the more it grabs you." She knelt down beside Jaime.

"Don't move," she said. She stroked the vines like you would stroke a cat. In a minute the vines seemed to relax. They let go of Jaime's legs.

"Thanks," he said. He stood up next to her. They were about the same height.

She smiled at him. Then she turned back to me. Her smile faded. "Your brother asked for your help. Why didn't you listen?"

I didn't know what to say. She made me feel bad. I didn't like this weird place. I wanted to go back home.

We continued down the path. Ría and Jaime walked ahead of me. I couldn't believe she liked that nerd better than me.

Finally, we reached a **clearing** in the trees. The forest stopped and a grassy hill began.

Heads Up!

How do you think Ría feels about Gilbert?
Why do you think she feels this way?

"You will meet our leader on the top of the hill," she said.

"What is he like?" Jaime asked her.

Ría said, "He is wise."

"If he is so wise, why can't he find food?" I asked. I was tired of her silly way of talking.

"I'm going this way," Ría said. "Come or not." She totally ignored my question. She just walked up the hill.

I was starting not to like this girl. Jaime fell into step behind her. I followed him. I didn't know where else to go.

The grass felt like a soft green carpet under my feet. What a change from that bumpy forest trail! I didn't have to look down at my feet anymore. So I looked up. And I saw a man standing before us. At least I think it was a man.

Heads Up!

Reread what Jaime says on page 13 about the snake-bird statue. Then think about the details of this new place. Where do you think Gilbert and Jaime might be?

Like Ría, this guy had a thing for feathers. He wore a feathered crown. A huge cape of feathers **draped** over his shoulders.

Ría dropped down on one knee. "Great leader, I bring visitors from far away."

Slowly he turned around. He had a dark face. His nose was straight. His chin was square. His eyes were like pieces of cold black glass.

"You are not welcome here. Leave or die."

6

Friends or Enemies?

I don't know who this leader guy is.
But you don't want to make him mad.

"Leave or die," the man said. That was an easy choice. "Leave." I opened my mouth to answer. But I was too scared. Nothing came out.

Then Jaime's voice rang out clear and strong. "We want to leave, great leader. But we don't know how. Can you help us?"

The leader blinked at little Jaime. "You show a brave face, little one. From what far away place have you come?"

I couldn't let that little shrimp make me look bad. So I swallowed hard and said, "It's a long story, leader. It's hard to explain."

The leader looked at me, then back at Jaime. "Are you gods?"

I wondered why everyone kept asking that.

"No, we're not gods. We're just two brothers who got sent here by mistake. It was all a mistake."

"Brothers?" The leader seemed to think about the word for a moment. Then he asked again, "From what place have you come?"

Jaime said, "We came from the flea market."

The leader frowned. "Where?"

Jaime began to speak. "You see, there was this old man—"

I slapped my hand over my brother's mouth. The whole "black mirror" thing had really upset Ría. I definitely didn't want to upset the leader.

But Ría spoke up. "They came through the black mirror."

I sighed, and then I let Jaime go.

"It had to be magic," Jaime said. "Or some kind of **curse**."

The leader rubbed his chin with his hand. He stared at my brother and me for a long moment.

—Heads Up!—

Compare and contrast how Gilbert and Jaime react to danger. Who is braver?

Then he said, "My brother carries the black mirror. You must have angered him."

"It was Gilbert. He broke a snake-bird statue," Jaime said.

I punched Jaime in the shoulder. "Tell it right. You pushed me. You made me drop it, creep."

"And you acted like I should pay for the whole thing!" Jaime started yelling. "And you lied about the money! You said you only had two dollars. But you really have ten. You're so **selfish**!"

"Stop!" The leader raised his hand. "This matter is between you and my brother." The leader's face looked very angry. "But you must go now. We cannot feed two more mouths. My people are starving."

"What do you want us to do about it?" I said without thinking.

"You're the leader," Jaime added. "Take care of your own people."

"Yeah," I said. I know it was weak. But I couldn't think of anything else.

"Silence!" The leader raised both his arms. His cape opened up. I realized it wasn't a cape at all. It was a set of wings.

"As ants, you brothers will learn a lesson. You will learn, or you will remain as small as your hearts."

Suddenly, I felt strange. I felt myself getting smaller and smaller. I felt legs popping out of my stomach. Two **feelers** poked out of my head. What was happening to me?

Heads Up!

The leader says the brothers will learn a lesson or "remain as small as their hearts." What lesson do you think the leader wants them to learn?

"As ants, you brothers will learn a lesson," the leader says.

Ant's-Eye View

Hey! How come I have six legs?

"Gilbert, is that you? You look like an ant."

I looked at Jaime. He had six legs with tiny hairs. He had a long black body and a tiny round head. He was so ugly.

"Hey, Gilbert, we're the same size. That's cool!"

"What did you say, dork? Did you happen to notice that we just got turned into ants?" I lifted my head. "And now, look! The sky turned green."

Jaime said, "It's just the grass, genius. Think about it. How small is an ant?"

"I'm glad you like being an ant so much. Now what do we do next? Do we go **raid** a picnic?"

"Ría's people are starving. So, I'm guessing there are no picnics."

"Okay, fine. So, then what are we supposed to do now?"

"Let's start walking. Maybe we can find some food on the ground or something."

I thought walking through the forest was rough. Try walking on six legs. I tripped on my arms. Were they my arms? They might have been my legs. I had so many it was hard to tell. I fell on my face over and over. Jaime had the same trouble. We were getting nowhere fast.

I was out of breath. "Say we finally figure out how to walk on six legs. How will we carry anything? We're ants!"

Jaime's ant head shook back and forth. "Ants can carry ten times their own weight. Some of us don't sleep through science class."

"Well, forget about going to any kind of class any more. 'Cause—guess what? We're just ants!"

"Well, I'm not going to give up. I don't want to be an ant all my life." Jaime tried walking again.

I had to admit it. Jaime was right. I couldn't look like a quitter. I tried harder. Pretty soon, my legs were working better. Both of us tripped. But we kept walking, my brother and I.

Everything looked so big. Dirt and sand were huge **boulders** to us. We had to climb over them.

Grass shot up from the ground. It looked as tall as trees to us.

We finally reached the end of the grass. A tree root looked like a giant brown snake.

Slowly we climbed the root. The roughness made all six of my feet sore. Finally we reached the top.

"Gilbert, look!" said Jaime.

"What?" I said. "It's just a seed."

"But you can plant a seed. If we take seeds back to the people, they can grow food," Jaime said. "And maybe if we help them, the leader will change us back into people. Then maybe he can **convince** his brother with the black mirror . . ."

I started walking toward the seed. That kid was always talking. Then everything got dark for a second. I looked up and saw a huge black crow. She was flying right for our seed.

Heads Up!

What do you think will happen next?

8

A Different Mirror

Jaime and I get a look at how others see us.
And we don't look too good.

The crow landed on the root and picked up the seed.

"Hey, wait!" I yelled. "We need that seed!"

Could ants talk to crows? I didn't know. But this was a pretty crazy place.

"We saw it first!" Jaime added.

"Who cares? I'm hungry," the crow said with the seed still in her beak.

"But we really need it," I said. "Look, it's a long story. But the truth is that we're not really ants."

I couldn't believe I was trying to explain this whole mess to a bird.

The crow just laughed. Then she flew away with our seed.

"Wow. That was so selfish!" I said out loud.

"I don't know," Jaime said. "But think about it. I bet that to Ría and her leader, we looked pretty selfish, too."

"And to the old man at the flea market," I sighed. "Maybe Ría was wrong. You *can* find yourself in a black mirror."

Suddenly, things were making a little more sense to me. "Come on, brother ant. We'll find another seed. At least now we know what we're looking for. Let's go!"

We didn't have to walk far. We saw another seed. But this one was moving.

"Follow that ant!" Jaime cried.

He was right. Underneath the seed was a big red ant. We took off after it.

"Hey, wait!" I yelled out.

The red ant looked at us and kept moving.

"Where can we find a seed like yours?" Jaime asked.

"It's **maize**," he grunted.

"What's maize?" I asked.

"It's an Aztec word for corn," Jaime told me.

"We need some maize, too," I said, out of breath from running on six legs.

The red ant said, "I'm taking this back to my nest. That is my job."

"Just one maize seed," I told it. "Come on, man. Don't be greedy."

"Go back to your nest," the red ant said.

"Come on," Jaime said. "Let's follow him."

Jaime and I walked over many, many rocks. Then we saw a tall mountain. Or was it only an anthill? To us, it seemed to touch the sky.

The red ant disappeared inside the mountain.

"Should we follow?" Jaime asked me.

I started to remember some things from science class. "Maybe it's their nest," I said. "If it is, there should be more seeds."

My brother and I crawled inside. It was dark. My legs were six times more tired than normal.

We finally reached a place where sunlight came in from the top. We stopped and stared. The room was filled with seeds. There were orange, black, yellow, and brown seeds. The ants must store their food here.

"We have to tell Ría and her leader about this," I said. "They could plant these seeds and have all the food they need."

"Gilbert, do you think they will believe us? I mean, we weren't very helpful before."

"You're right," I said. "I'll carry some seeds back. I'm strong."

"I'll carry one, too," Jaime said.

"I'm bigger than you, squirt," I reminded him.

"Not any more. We're both the same size now."

"I'll show you," I said. I crawled over to a yellow seed. I tried to lift the seed with my back legs. It was very heavy. I pushed it on my back.

"See? I can do it," I said. The corn seed fell on top of me. And I couldn't breathe.

Heads Up!

Is Gilbert's attitude toward his brother changing? Explain.

9

Teamwork

It takes two to get this seed moving.

I looked at my brother. I had to admit the truth. I couldn't lift the seed.

"Help," I croaked.

"Not to worry," said my brother the ant. "We'll carry it together."

He helped me raise the seed. Then we tried to carry it together. But we didn't get far.

"We each have six legs," Jaime said. "That's way more than we need."

"You're right. Let's use some more of our legs or arms for the seed."

We tried to walk on two legs. But we both fell over. I'm sure we looked silly. We were two ants, but we didn't know how to carry a seed.

"This isn't working," Jaime said. "Help me push the seed onto this leaf."

"What a waste of time," was what I almost said. But then I thought about it. "Good idea, bro. I see what you mean."

Then he grabbed the leaf with his mouth. I did the same. And we started dragging the leaf and the seed toward the light. It wasn't exactly smooth sailing. But we were working together. Or at least we were for a while.

Now an army of red ants were lining up in front of us. They blocked the way. They didn't want us stealing their food.

"What do we do?" Jaime asked.

"I don't know, little bro," I answered. "I really don't. You're the genius. I like baseball."

Out of the light came a rush of air. We felt it move us.

"Jaime, don't let go of the seed. No matter what. Ría's people need it to live."

We saw a birdlike creature with a man's face and a feathered crown. Its colorful wings moved the air around us. The bird man scooped us up before we could even scream. His dark hands carried my brother and me. Somehow we held on to the seed.

The bird man flew us up into the sunlight. We flew through blue skies. It was scary. But it was also kind of cool.

We landed on the same hill as before. Ría stood there with her hand out. We were dropped gently into her palm.

We saw the winged creature land beside her. There was a **shimmer** of light. Then he changed into a man. It was Ría's leader.

"You have done well as brothers," he said. "And you have done something for my people." He waved his hand over us.

Suddenly, I felt strange. I was falling through space. When I landed I was me again. I stood beside Jaime. I looked into his familiar face and smiled. "Good to see you again, *hermano*."

He smiled at me. "I'm so glad to have two legs again. I don't even mind being short."

—Heads Up!—

"Hermano" means brother in Spanish. Do you think that Gilbert would have called Jaime "hermano" before they were ants?

The brothers hold on to the seed tightly.

I punched my brother's shoulder in a playful way. Then I turned to the leader. "Here is a maize seed for your people." I held it in my hand. It looked so tiny. How could it have been so heavy?

"The ants in the nest at the bottom of the hill will be happy to share some more of them with you," I told him.

It was not exactly true. But it would serve those greedy ants right!

The leader nodded his head. "The people will learn from the earth. They will grow strong. You are friends to our people. We will tell this story about two brothers from this time forward."

"Thanks," I said. "But we still need to find our way home."

"You have great magic, leader." Jaime bowed deep from the waist. "Will you take us back where we belong?"

"No." The leader shook his head. "I cannot help you."

10

The Black Lake

My brother and I have to find our own way back home.

I couldn't believe my ears. "You won't help us? But we helped you."

"The black mirror sent you here," he said. "Only its magic can take you back."

Jaime and I looked at each other. "Now what?" we said at the same time.

Ría placed one hand on my shoulder. She put the other on Jaime's shoulder. "You are brothers. Listen to each other."

Jamie nodded. "Okay, the old man said we had to find a new path."

I could see Jaime was thinking out loud. I started to think, too. "We were on a rocky path that twisted and turned like a snake. We need to find a better path. That's what he said."

Jaime looked around. "There!" he said.

I turned where my brother pointed. A soft green trail went off in a straight line. In the distance I thought I saw a lake. "That's it." I started to take off. Then I stopped and turned back to Ría and the leader.

"Thank you for helping us," I said.

"Yes," Jaime said. "Thanks!"

She gave us a smile. "You helped us too. Stay strong as brothers."

I wished she could have come with us. But I knew that she belonged here. And we had to find our way home.

"Let's go, Gilbert," my brother said. "Let's follow that path."

I bowed to the leader and waved at Ría. Then my brother and I ran down the trail toward the lake. Would it lead us home?

Heads Up!

How are the two paths in this story like the relationship between Gilbert and Jaime? Do the paths help show how the brothers have changed? Explain.

We laughed with hope and excitement. We got to the edge. Then both of us went, "Huh?"

"Wow! Look!" Jaime cried out.

I stared into the lake in **disbelief.** The water wasn't blue, or even green. It was black. Weird.

Jaime stared down at the lake. After a long moment he said, "This looks like a giant black mirror, right Gilbert?"

It did. And Ría's leader told us that only the black mirror could take us back. Was this it? Was this our way home? I wasn't sure. And I was worried. I knew Jaime couldn't swim too well.

"I think we should jump in, Gilbert." Jaime's voice was quiet and calm.

I smiled at my little brother. He was a brave little guy. I reached out my hand to Jaime. He grabbed it. Together we called out, "One, two, three, jump!"

Will the brothers find their way back home?

11

Mirror, Mirror

**What a weird adventure. I have to admit,
I'm glad Jaime was around to share it.**

We never felt any water. It was like a cool, smooth darkness covering us. But it didn't feel wet at all. Our hands slipped apart. But I knew my brother was still with me.

Something bright hit my eyes. I started blinking. The **glare** made my eyes water. It was from the sun. It was bouncing off a shiny mirror.

Jaime and I were back at the flea market. We were standing at the old man's truck. We stared at our own smiling faces. We were looking into a mirror.

The old man held the mirror. I noticed his dark fingers. He wore a single ring with a silver bird carved on it. The bird had a man's face. On its head was a crown of feathers.

I stepped back. I turned to look at Jaime.

Jaime had started to smile at me. Then he stopped smiling.

I knew what he was thinking. Had we been here the whole time? What if nothing had happened? Was any of it real?

I looked at the ground. The broken statue lay at our feet. I looked back into the old man's face. His black eyes seemed to stare right through me.

I said, "I'm sorry for breaking your statue." Then I bent down. I started to pick up the pieces.

"It was my fault, too," my brother said. He bent down and helped me.

We put the broken pieces on the table.

"Accidents happen," the old man said to us. "There is a family up the hill. They roast corn to sell. Will you buy me one? It tastes so good."

"Sure," I said. "Is that all we can do?" I asked.

"Yes," he said. "I'm very hungry."

We walked up the hill and saw a young girl selling corn. She had black shiny hair. She wore a white blouse. Tiny birds decorated the collar.

I pulled out my money. Jaime did, too.

Jaime said, "Here. I'll give you half."

"You two must be brothers." She smiled and handed us the roasted corn. It was wrapped inside paper towels. It smelled delicious.

Then we walked back to the spot where the rock path had been. But here's the really strange part. There was no path. There was no tree, no truck, and no old man. There weren't even any tire tracks on the soft green grass.

"He's gone," Jaime said. "It must be a mystery from history."

I looked at my brother. My brother always said the dumbest—I stopped myself right in the middle of that thought.

Then Jaime said, "Do you want to know what I think, Gilbert?"

"What, *hermano*?" I said, messing up his hair.

Heads Up!

Gilbert starts to get angry at Jaime. Why do you think he stops himself?

"I think we should buy Mom a mirror. Do you think she'd like that?" he asked.

I couldn't help but grin. "That'll be a good present for her, Jaime. I have nine dollars left. Let's try to find a really pretty one before it's time to meet Uncle Tulio."

And we walked down the hill together.

Heads Up!

Notice how Jaime and Gilbert have changed. What lesson do you think the brothers learned?

Meet the Author

Diane Gonzales Bertrand

Diane Gonzales Bertrand was raised in a family of seven children. Diane and her **siblings** were regular visitors to the public library because it didn't cost any money. Diane loved books and wrote stories, essays, and poems. She even wrote a novel when she was in fifth grade.

Today, Diane is a teacher and a professional writer. Some of her novels include *Sweet Fifteen, Trino's Choice,* and its sequel, *Trino's Time.* She is currently working on two new novels.

Diane says that she got the idea for *Black Mirror* from her two children, Nick and Suzanne. Nick suggested that she base her story on the Aztec legend of Quetzalcóatl. He turned into an ant to bring corn to his people.

When Diane went to the library to find out more about the legend, she discovered that Quetzalcóatl had a brother named Tezcatlipoca. And they didn't get along. She also learned that Tezcatlipoca carried a black mirror. She put those elements together and wrote her very first fantasy novel.

Glossary

admire *(verb)* to look at something and enjoy it, or to like and respect someone (p. 21)

bargain *(noun)* a good price (p. 12)

boulder *(noun)* a huge rock (p. 34)

clearing *(noun)* a place in the middle of a forest where there are no trees (p. 25)

concentrate *(verb)* to focus on (p. 23)

convince *(verb)* to persuade someone to believe you (p. 35)

curse *(noun)* an evil spell intended to hurt someone (p. 29)

disbelief *(noun)* a refusal to believe something is true (p. 47)

drape *(verb)* to hang loosely over (p. 27)

feeler *(noun)* an antenna on the head of an insect (p. 31)

glare *(noun)* a very bright light (p. 49)

maize *(noun)* corn (p. 37)

path *(noun)* a trail or route for walking; a plan for living your life (p. 9)

Glossary

raid *(verb)* to attack by surprise (p. 33)

seek *(verb)* to look for (p. 20)

selfish *(adjective)* caring only about yourself; not thinking of others (p. 30)

shimmer *(noun)* a faint, unsteady light (p. 42)

sibling *(noun)* a brother or sister (p. 53)

sling *(verb)* to throw like you're throwing from a slingshot; to fling (p. 20)

towering *(adjective)* very tall; taller than other things nearby (p. 7)

unique *(adjective)* unlike anything else (p. 10)